Uno.

A little bar, owned by an old Italia~~n~~ ~~at~~ the end of a very long and dar~~k~~ ~~street~~ ~~...~~ of Manhattan. This partic~~ular~~ ~~bar was~~ ~~...~~ the ordinary. It was unassuming a~~nd~~ ~~...~~ ~~a~~part from a little, elderly Spanish lady. 'L'~~il Miss Rosa~~, ~~s~~he was fondly nicknamed by the family. She wa~~s~~, ~~a~~most nights, at her regular spot at the end of the bar, always with a cigarette clutched between her fingers and accompanied by a glass of Jerez over ice. She was now, possibly, in her eighties and always ended the night slumped over her empty glass, her fourth or fifth of the night, in an unladylike manner – crying over memories that she repeated to any unfortunate ear that was close enough to feel obliged to listen to it. When Stefano, the father, closed his bar for the night he would always offer to walk L'il Miss Rosa next door to her one bedroomed apartment that was situated on the sixth floor of a rundown tenement building which had a view over the Hudson river. Every time she would thank him but kindly refuse. She tried hard to keep away from the men of New York, as she had done in Madrid thirty years before and used her woeful, self-blaming story as her reason.

***

Lucia woke up before the sun rose over the silhouetted mountains as she always did at the same time each morning. There seemed little need to wake up any more. If it wasn't for her only remaining son, she would sleep at the next sunset and choose never to see another sunrise. However, her son Vicente, her remaining reason for life, continued his daily chores in the fields out on the plain and, as such, she lived out the last few years of her life.

She often recalled her first affectionate memories with her husband around this time of the day. Passionate seasons in the vineyards and orange groves – she, laying down, staring up at her husband whose sturdy, sun bleached arms held him up above her whilst the sun pounded his back as they caressed.

Shortly after their wedding day, her husband took her to Sevilla to the bullfight. At such a naïve, young age – Lucia found the fight terrifying, whilst her love heckled the bull and cheered when the sword pierced the beast's spine – forcing it to slump down in the dust in defeat, exhausted from the long chase and humiliated by the matador's victory. Blood oozed from the creature's wounds as its breathing shortened and eventually stopped. Although Lucia buried her face in her husband's chest

with horror, she felt a surge of passion from the occasion and a sudden lust for this man, as he whispered to her: "la agonía es larga pero la muerte es segura"(1).

Vicente was already putting together his tools for another long day in the field tending to the oranges. Lucia gave him a long stare before crossing to the window to glare out at the mountains.

"So, off again?" Lucia asked her son, still staring out the window.

"Mother the oranges need tending, you know this. You cannot keep me here and let the trees wilt, even if you wanted to."

Suddenly, Lucia snapped out of her daze and faced her son. "Wait, let me make you lunch and give you some water."

"It's fine. I must go. I shall eat oranges. - please pass me the knife."

"Damn this knife", she began, muttering under her breath. "Damn all knives – and the man that invented them. Such a small thing a baby or an old woman like me can use to destroy lives and stop a heartbeat. A mere blade, such a trivial looking thing that can ruin a family."

Vicente looked away to finish his pack for the fields. "Please let's change the subject", he begged. This was a recurring topic that haunted his mother since the death of his father and brother, which had been over fifteen years ago, an issue that he had to listen to nearly everyday ever since.

His mother stood and held the knife in her hands, playing with the simple design of the instrument.

"I'm sorry, son. I know, I know – it is venom that is in my mouth that I need to purge. I need to devote my life to you now. But I can't, I just cannot. I was expecting to enjoy the best things in life with my husband, your father, for many more years yet - and see your brother bring me many a grandson and granddaughter. Now I rely solely upon you to bless your new bride and to bring me this gift to continue the Lorca bloodline."

Once packed, Vicente merely dropped a kiss upon his mother's forehead before flinging himself out the front door and out into the mid morning sun. As she closed the door behind him, Lucia whispered, "la agonía es larga pero la muerte es segura"(1).

Outside, a majestic winged predator hovered above a clump of dry bushes, eyes upon an ignorant creature scourging the desolate terrain for food in the daylight. Suddenly it flung itself down on the helpless hare and dragged it back into the air, tearing at its body with a dagger sharp beak as it ripped into the flesh, crying out as a sign of victory.

1. *Nothing lasts forever*

***

Lucia pottered, for what seemed like hours, around the home. In keeping with her daily routines, she tried to bake bread, tried to dry the sheets, tried to turn the oranges to marmalade or ferment the red juicy grapes. All of these attempts were hopeless. For most, the hot, still heat of the August sun was an excuse for their sense of lethargy. For Lucia everything just seemed trivial. Her existence seemed trivial. One thing she could bring herself to do was squeeze her rosary and recite prayers for her lost husband and son, while turning her back to the room and speaking whispers to the wall like a mad woman.

She was abruptly interrupted when, at midday, the woman from the neighbouring farm came in, breaking Lucia's meditative state.

"If I was never to see another mouse again and God were to expel them from Andalucia I would live my days out in peace and comfort". Maria José, the neighbour – short, stocky and at a similar age to Lucia, took a place at the table, pulled out a black fan with white, small flowers entwined into its pattern and violently swayed it to and fro to disturb the arid heat.

"Our corn is ruined, bags split in our old stables and spilt everywhere! And God damn this heat."

"Take some water", advised Lucia as she decanted some into a clay mug for her friend.

Maria José took a long drink and let out a deep sigh.

"Any sign of the girl yet, Lucia?", asked Maria José.

"I have not seen her. The family have dwellings on the road between here and the mountains. On the other side of the river. She is beautiful, I am told. Dark, passionate eyes and black hair often braided. Thin, but Vicente insists that she has potential to bear children."

"She will bring you both such beautiful children. With your son's physique I will pray for a bounty of strong, powerful boys to help tend the fields", Maria José insisted.

A long silence passed between the two women, a serene, abnormally long silence - filled with the hot, dry heat of the midday air.

"How long has Vicente known this girl?"

Lucia shot her neighbour a short stare and then eyed the mountains in the distance. "Three years",

Lucia declared. "I have heard she had another lover prior to my son too. This I know very little about."

"I have heard things", started Maria José, "but you can't say anyone knows her well. She lives with her father, way off, miles from the nearest house, like you said. But she's a good girl. Accustomed to solitude."

This startled Lucia. How could someone know her sons fiancé more than her? She never had the opportunity to meet the girl and Vicente kept the knowledge of her very private, like a love struck adolescent, who would pine over his first ever lover. She knew not of her father, nor her aptitude, her grace, her charm, her personality, merely what was revealed in a portrait photograph of her – with a melancholy face and her dark, wavy hair that flowed freely over her shoulders.

"Ah! The things people know!", Lucia replied, hiding her anguish of her neighbour's superior knowledge.

She couldn't hold her tongue. She needed to know what her future daughter in law's mother was like: "and the mother, do you have much knowledge of her?"

"A truly beautiful woman, so I understand. Dead now. Her face shone like a saint's; but she would not be to my liking. She didn't love her husband, or so people say. I know nothing of whether she was a decent woman or not, but she was proud. I pray that her beauty and pride is reflected in your son's fiancé."

All of a sudden Maria José recalled an important scrap of gossip but held her tongue – for though she would bask in the joy of spreading it, in that moment she saw how her beloved neighbour would act if she knew. She, for a mere second envisioned how Lucia would become enraged. What ceramic plates she may smash, what furniture would be overturned or red wine splashed against the white washed walls – in her fury of discovering some truths about the bride to be. The fiancés mere association with the house of Felix, the family that murdered Lucia's husband and eldest son would turn the saliva into bile within her mouth. At this indecision, Maria José stayed silent, unnaturally silent for a woman who usually filled empty space with gossip and rumours.

Outside a woodcutter travelled down the dusty road beyond the clump of bushes and a withering single pine tree, muttering to himself whilst his exhausted mule tugged a hefty load of wood behind her, back-broken in the heat, eyes rolling back and gurning to amplify her distress and aching bones, with withered muscles and bruised body – wrecked by the seemingly endless years of pain and work, pain and work, pain and work.

"Why the silence woman?", Lucia seemed to demand, rather than ask. She knew her friend too well to understand the unnatural element of a break in a conversation.

Maria José poised, too eager to reveal what she knew. Still, "nothing", she lied, the truth tucked away behind her tongue.

The truth was, the woman betrothed to Vicente had in fact been either a lover or a childhood sweetheart, as Maria José couldn't quite recall from a source of gossip she had once heard (neither of which would have made any difference in Lucia's eyes), of the youngest son of the pack of Felix who murdered Lucia's son and husband in broad day light, out in their field amongst the oranges, leaving the scene with a mixture of father and son's blood seeping down into the very roots of the orange grove. Admiration for a man who was a mere baby when this happened would curdle Lucia's stomach. Tongues were supposed to be held, for the sake of the lovers and the old mother's contempt. She knew that in her friend's eyes, no matter how innocent a part the former lover played in the death of Lucia's husband and son, "De tal palo, tal astilla" (2).

As Maria José left the house, she bypassed the woodcutter on the path, flogging and kicking his mule – too exhausted to continue with her heavy burden, eyes weeping in the midday sun.

2. *From such a stick, such a splinter.*

***

Far north from there, somewhere between the bustling, industrial city of Bilbao and the foothills of the Pyrenees lay a small village on the coast. A grievous event had taken place a few days ago which had each villager left bewildered.

The subconscious, such a powerful and controlling tool, had taken over the mind of a certain beautiful yet naïve woman – who had been kept within a controlling marriage for only six months. This particular woman had, unwillingly and almost completely unaware, grown fond of her cousin, who she had always considered an innocent playmate as a child, since her wedding day. Now at the age of seventeen, her feelings had turned much stronger. Their mutual desires between one another had become raw and dark and deeply shameful. On one particular night, when the moon's reflection bounced gently on the calm ocean, the lovers were discovered, clasped in each other's arms, with nothing but a sheet covering them in the marriage bed. In a fit of rage, the husband dragged the cousin by the hair and shot him twice in the back. As for the wife - he repeatedly kicked her, beat her and then smothered her with the same pillow that had cushioned the lovers heads throughout the night. Early the next morning, the husband, with a head throbbing with the effect of alcohol but a mind caged in fury, tossed the bodies into a poorly constructed grave which was deep but too short for each corpse to lie in. As the moist earth started to cover the naked bodies, the woman started to regain consciousness but the earth, shovelled onto her by the furious husband, ensured that she would be forever shrouded in darkness.

Dos.

Vicente eyed the spot every day, first thing in the morning and last in the evening, like a torture recalling every element of that day, reciting the memories of his blurred vision as he ran from the bodies with naïve innocence, his heart pounding and his breath heaving. He remembered blood seeping from the open stab wounds, drenching white shirts with a deep vermilion, his father's eyes rolling back into their sockets, as he lived the last few painful seconds of his life, whilst his brother laid opposite, face down in the bloody soil. Like a curse, this plot of land, that now seemed no different from the rest of the field to any other person's eyes, had a hold on Vicente, making him envision the soulless bodies as if the murder had just happened. Something evil lurked within the soil there. As if the ground were tainted with the memory of the deaths, few trees bore fruit nearby – and if they did, the fruit was sour and rotted quickly whilst their branches appeared withered and spindly with leaves which fell much sooner than other trees.

***

In the town there was a square. It wasn't the town's Plaza Major. This square didn't have an elegant fountain that flowed with cool, fresh water. Nor a bounty of tavernas which surrounded the fountain. This square wasn't worthy of the town's old church sitting proudly for all the townspeople to look at, to worship and to admire. This particular square didn't have so much as a single tree to adorn it, unlike the twelve acacia trees which bloomed a vibrant yellow every summer to boast the Plaza Major's splendour. This square sat behind its sumptuous equivalent, shrouded in a shadow cast by the gaunt houses that squatted around it. Nestled in the corner of this particular square was a little three storey house, once painted in a bright, lemon yellow but now showing signs of its age, with plaster slowly crumbling away to reveal the bricks underneath. Its shutters rarely opened, winter or summer – as if the house was holding a secret deep within or hiding from the eyes that were outside. A crudely built stable was added to the side of the house with a meagre amount of straw.

A mother sat on the edge of her bed, hopelessly attempting to sing her baby daughter to sleep. The baby whined – bothered by the discomfort from the endless heat.

The room was very sparsely decorated. The big, iron-framed bed took up most of the room. A thin, dark wooden wardrobe cowered in the corner and a table covered in lace stood at the foot of the bed, bearing a vase with several yellow carnation flowers.

The mother pushed a reckless strand of hair behind her ear and continued her song. She was a dainty, young woman with very unusual blonde hair, tightly tied in to a bun. The truth was, the heat troubled her too. Every year, this region at the foot of the mountains that lay on the plains was prone to this landlocked heat, but she could never get used to it. It tormented the people of the town all day and didn't cease until the early hours of the morning. She would have loved for someone to caress her or care about her discomfort as she did for her own child. To cry and wail, to confide in someone else the one thousand concerns that spun round in her head.

A clatter came from downstairs from the door that led in off the street, which startled the young woman.

"Leonardo?", the mother called. She knew that, although it would give her slight comfort to know it was him that had entered off the street and not a thief or a drunkard, both of which were possible in this square and the domiciles that surrounded it late in the afternoon, he would not honour her with a response, merely his presence in the room would relieve her when he came upstairs to 'check up' on his wife and the new born baby.

"Where were you? You have been gone all day", She asked her husband, at the same time worried and relieved.

"The damn stallion needed shoeing again. The cost of that animal!"

He came up close and placed a tepid kiss indifferently on his child's forehead and brushed his wife's strand of hair, that had come loose again, back behind her ear. Leonardo was a handsome, dark and strong man, in his mid thirties, very different from his wife. He had thick black hair which led from his side burns into a shadow-like stubble surrounding his chin. His eyes were dark chocolate and had a mysterious depth to them and his hands were big and strong and unnaturally smooth and soft.

The door latch downstairs clicked open again and an old wizened woman, mother to Leonardo's wife, huffed her way up the staircase. This woman had a similar stature to her daughter who she ignored when she came into the bedroom but, instead, gave Leonardo a hard, pensive and vaguely mistrusting stare.

"That beast is close to death", she exclaimed as she set herself down beside her daughter. "How is it in that much of a lather? You say that you don't ride it past the fields. How is it close to death if it only does its regular chores with you?"

Her distaste for her daughter's husband was combined with suspicion. It made both Leonardo and his wife feel uneasy, though she thought exactly the same as her mother, she would not dare be as brash.

"The beast is old", Leonardo falsely confessed, "and it is little use to me in these fields any more. Hungry dogs would make more use of it that I can these days."

With an attempt to either clear the air of scepticism or unburden her husband of the spotlight, the young mother rose her voice to exclaim: "Rosa is to be married!"

At this point, Leonardo had opened the shutters, only very slightly and had his forehead lent on his right arm, looking out of the bedroom's tiny window at the almost vacant square beneath him and let out a sigh as a response, along with a flat, unenthusiastic: "si?"

"Yes to a widow's only son. You know, the widow Lorca, the señora who's son was killed by ..."

The girl stopped dead and looked up from her child at her mother who was glaring at her.

She didn't know how this snippet of information had escaped her mouth so carelessly and inarticulately. As the couple rarely spoke any more, it was almost as if she, the wife, was forgetting who her husband was.

"… my siblings", Leonardo replied, shamelessly and still flatly, finishing her sentence – his eyes still fixed on the square.

His wife, who was one of of many second cousins to Rosa on her father's side of the family, had never met her husband's three brothers. She knew about them, of course. The whole town knew about them, the terrible Felix family, and the devastating murder that they committed, but to her, they were still strangers. Leonardo talked very little to her, and even less about his family.

Abruptly, Leonardo doubled back and left the house, muttering that he was 'going out' to whoever heard him. Both women were left wondering as to why. Had he felt embarrassed or ashamed or angry at his wife's words? Ultimately, the young wife was sure it was her doing that made him go back outside so quickly, as she held back tears in her mother's presence.

Tres.

Saying that the road to the bridesmaid's house was bumpy would have been a considerable understatement. The old plough horse pulled the cart that viciously rocked over the dirt track heading west, through a barren landscape that was only occasionally dotted with bushes and pomegranate trees.

Lucia sat in the back of the cart, flapping her black laced fan vigorously whilst sighing and groaning in discomfort. She wore her usual black, mourning attire, complete with her mantilla and appeared like a dark, unfriendly silhouette being pulled along through the landscape. Vicente led the troubled creature on foot, tugging at its rein as it stepped over the dried up soil. The scrubby land slowly gave way to a sprawl of alfalfa and a vineyard, which heralded the distant view of the father-in-law's cortijo. Close to the building a variety of chickens scratched around the front of the house. Several pigs lay in the parched mud that had turned into dried up dirt by the blistering sun in a little pen that was fixed to the side of the house and a dozen skeletal cows, adorned with bell-belts, scoured a nearby field for vegetation.

Vicente was astonished. Along the journey he had felt fearful of his mother's opinions: what would she think about the desolate appearance of the nearby landscape, how would she complain about the rough dirt track that led up to the father-in-law's house and, most importantly – what opinion would she express about the fiancé? He knew himself that the cortijo wasn't a promising spectacle, with its starved animals and parched land – but his mother remained silent. Her face appeared more intrigued than judgemental as they pulled up to the house.

A woman wearing a cream linen apron on top of a charcoal grey shift dress answered the door.

"We are here to see señor Machado and my, soon to be, daughter-in-law", Lucia exclaimed in a proud voice. In the doorway, her son stood behind her, his tall, thin physique shadowed the sunlight. The woman who answered the door was a petite, mousy creature with very tanned skin with a wary, mistrustful look on her face. She did not smile, nor did she open the door wide enough to suggest a welcoming invitation into the house, however she slowly creaked the door open wide enough to let them both in.

"Come", she muttered, as she disappeared into the darkness of the house to fetch her master.

The house was far grander than the exterior would suggest. Two stag heads stared blankly at each other from either side of the room, mounted on a wall which was white washed but adorned in portraits and old photographs. One photo depicted, Lucia assumed, the 'family' - Rosa, her father and her mother. Rosa stood to the left of the picture, dressed in a pinstriped shift dress and her mother sat in a chair in the centre, staring straight at the photographer with melancholic grace, with her husband standing directly behind her. The thing that intrigued Lucia the most was Rosa, who stood with her hands clasped together in front of her, but her attention was focused on something outside of the picture, which made her smile in a very mischievous way.

Two luxurious, antique armchairs sat beside a fire place, facing one another, with a heavy, oak table between them which held a ceramic jug of rich, red wine and four matching ceramic cups. There was also an old wooden bench that sat at the opposite end of the room against the wall. All of these items were placed proudly on a thick, red rug with intricate floral detail.

The mother and son stood in the room expectantly for a few minutes before the father strode in to greet them. He was a little taller than Lucia, with a thick, grey handlebar moustache and a receding hairline. He wore a dark grey jacket and a black tie that was wrapped tightly around his neck.

"It is an honour to have you in this house", the man proclaimed after politely reaching for Lucia's hand and kissing it. "Come take a seat and let's toast to our hijos!"

The father-in-law and Lucia both took a cup of wine and sat in the armchairs. Vicente did so too but lingered behind his mother's armchair, resting his hand on her shoulder.

"May I begin with a whole-hearted apology for the rough journey you will have endured to get to our cortijo", señor Machado apologised. "As is a justice from God that two betrothed families must endure that hideous road and the distances between the two houses. The path, combined with that wicked, rocky terrain and this terrible heat makes it more of an arduous mission to bring us together, and for this – I thank you."

Lucia seemed in awe by the gentleman's flattery and apologetic attitude and, for the first time that Vicente could remember, she replied with a genuine smile and fluttered her fan.

"Well, I assume that the arduous journey will be worth it. I know little of your daughter, señor, but from what I have seen from your pictures – she is quite beautiful", Lucia gestured to the wall with her closed fan, "and we should all be blessed with a bounty of beautiful grand children soon after this wedding."

"I thank you señora", said the old man. "I can assure you this is the hope of myself and my only daughter as well and, as such, this will be the case. I am proud of my daughter. In addition with her beauty and charm she is also humble and hard working. She shows devotion to her father and this house and I am sure she shall do the same with her husband and her mother-in-law, I have no doubt about that! I also have no doubts about the wedding taking place as soon as possible."

Lucia eyed the wall and its pictures.

"Nor do I", she said, "though I would have preferred to know more about your daughter. My son is completely smitten with her and assures me, as you have done señor, that she will make a decent wife. They have been courting for a while and I blame this God forsaken distance between us as to why I have not come sooner. But fate is fate and it must be endured."

At that moment, the daughter-in-law entered the room, hands clutching one another in front of her. Lucia rose from her seat and placed a kiss upon Rosa's forehead.

"Bless you my daughter, you really are more beautiful than any picture can express!" Indeed, she was. Her eyes were dark and mysterious and her slim figure gave way to ample hips and a curvaceous chest.

"Thank you madre", Rosa replied. "I am so happy to see you at last." Although Rosa flashed a brief smile while she spoke, her face seemed to resemble her mother's air of melancholia, which was depicted in the photographs – very dissimilar to the mischievous look that she had as a child.

"Vicente, my hijo", ordered his mother. "Take your fiancé elsewhere to talk further, as we now need to discuss arrangements for your wedding day!"

Cuatro.

The maid poured freshly boiled water into a tin bath for Rosa. The sun had only recently set into the dark, star-filled sky and Rosa stared out of the window contemplating her day.

"Maria?", Rosa questioned the maid, "what do you think of my soon to be mother-in-law?"

Maria, without looking away from her chores, shrugged. "Decent enough I suppose. Filled with pride, filled with obsession for her son, but decent enough. Why? If you love your fiancé you can surely overlook her airs."

"She seemed warmer to me than I had thought. I don't trust that. She had never met me and knows so little about both me and father. Vicente warned me that she was untrusting and difficult to please, but this was not the woman who came to our cortijo."

Maria sighed. "Maybe her son's love for you has overcome her mistrust in you? I am not one to know much about this sort of thing, but I could see that your fiancé is truly in love with you, while the parents were negotiating the wedding."

"Its not true love. We have been courting for three years and he asks very little about me. He is infatuated with my looks and my eyes and the dimples in my cheeks and my lace gowns and how it is odd how I drink water instead of wine or how there is a single freckle on my wrist. But he has never asked anything about this household or my mother." With this, Maria didn't know what to say or suggest. It was not her place to put forward her opinion, however much she'd have liked to.

Dull-eyed, Rosa turned and plunged herself into the water.

"Rosa!!", cried Maria, "the water is far too hot and not ready!"

Rosa seemed unaware of her maid's concerns and kept her eyes forward. In the distance, the faint noise of a racing horse could be heard. It appeared to get louder and louder until it stopped just a short distance from the house. The rider neither ventured further nor got off his horse, he just gazed at Rosa's window, hoping to see her. The mere sight of this young woman was sufficient to keep him happy all the way back to the town. So there he stayed, like a ghostly silhouette, looking up hopefully at the window. Finally, Rosa rose from her bath and went to the window and the figure stood there for a little while, completely shrouded in the darkness so's not to be seen, then, as Rosa's gas lamp went off, he turned and raced back.

***

That same night, Lucia had a dream. In this dream she was shrouded in darkness in the house of señor Machado and his daughter, only it was empty and much darker than it had been that day. The only things that she could see were the stags' heads mounted on the walls facing each other. But they were not dead. They were groaning and shrieking, flailing their antlers in a ferocious display, as if they wanted to fight each other, but were held back from doing so. Then, all of a sudden, they went deathly quiet and turned to face Lucia, or rather, to face something or someone behind her. As she turned she saw her son's fiancé. She looked more beautiful than she had done earlier that day – if such a thing was possible. Her hair was free and fell abundantly over her shoulder in dark wavy locks. She displayed a sincere, saddened look upon her face and held a bunch of wilting carnations with both hands. She wore her bridal gown, decorated in tiny, floral detailing and used her veil to attempt to mask her unhappiness. It even seemed as though the bride was crying.

Then, slowly, from the hem of her dress upward, crept a deep red, staining her dress as it grew. Too vibrant for the colour of wine, more like the colour of blood that had recently been drawn. As it grew close to her chest her face changed; less saddened and now a little more complacent, satisfied and then eventually joyful – letting out a surreal, almost cynical laugh that made Lucia feel extremely unnerved.

At the bride's feet lay the two stags, drenched in their own blood and gasping for their final breaths before their breathing ceased and all went dark.

Lucia struggled herself awake and gasped heavily as if she had just come out of a lagoon for air. Her eyes peered around the room as if uncertain whether she was still dreaming or not. She pulled herself from her bed, her night dress soaked with sweat, clinging to her back. She crept to the veranda and stared at the moon, taunting her with a full beam that identified every wrinkle in her aged skin.

***

Later that morning, Vicente came downstairs to find his mother slumped down against the door frame of the entrance to the house, the old oak door left wide open.

"Dios mio, mother! Are you okay?", he questioned, bewildered and concerned.

Lucia's eyes were slightly open, gazing at the horizon that shimmered with the baking heat that rose before it.

"Tell me, son. My dear, dear son. What do you know of your fiancé?", She asked, eyes unmoving.

Vicente staggered back a few steps, relieved that she was unharmed, but yet confused and concerned that she brought about this question so early on in the day.

"What an odd question to ask …! Well, many things. I know that she is kind and beautiful and will make a wonderful wife and daughter for yourself. I know that …"

"What of her family?", Lucia cut him short.

"Well … you have met señor Machado of course", He responded.

"And her mother, what of her? And her love life before you. Had she any other lovers?"

"Not that I know of", Vicente confessed.

Lucia turned her head to face him, her eyes deep with love for her last remaining child, and took his hand in hers.

"Find out for me, would you? If not for me then for yourself. I am certain that she is a good child. But I need to know that she will be a good wife too. Will you do that for me? Forget the fields today. Ride over to the house of señor Machado and take your fiancé for a walk."

Vicente sighed and bent down to the level of his mother.

"I will mama, if I cannot today then I definitely shall within the week." With that he helped his mother up and took her inside.

Cinco.

Some evenings later, Leonardo made his pilgrimage to the House of Rosa Machado, using the cover of darkness as both his excuse and his shield. At night he couldn't be seen and feel the shame of desiring a woman who could never be his. His black horse never got closer than about fifty feet to the cortijo's entrance, but just close enough for Leonardo to gaze up at the top left window and watch the silhouette of his desire glide around her room. There he would stay, even after her gas lamp had been put out, maybe for hours at a time, without a thought for his newborn child nor his wife. Eventually he would sigh deeply and race back to the town, with the anticipation of his return the following night.

***

That next day Vicente rode up to his fiancé's cortijo. Rosa was crocheting under the shade of an old, withered apple tree with her back to him. He crept up to her, like a mischievous boy and jerked both of his hands under her armpits to make her jump.

"I'm so sorry my love", Vicente said, "I couldn't help myself. I hope I didn't startle you too much."

"You did rather! It's fortunate for you that you are you and not someone else or this crochet needle would be the death of you!" She looked up a him and gave him a faint smile. He, in turn wrapped his long arms around her, squeezed her and let out a complacent sigh.

"Only a few more days until I can be with you for the rest of my life", exclaimed Vicente, his eyes gleaming optimistically behind his circular framed spectacles.

"Only two more days until the happiest day of our lives", she replied.

"Well, it will be one of the happiest days, at least", he laughed. "I will be happy each morning I wake up with you, each son you bare, every kiss we exchange. You will make me the happiest man in this country!"

With that, Vicente took his woman by the hand and led her behind the cortijo and down into a small patch of woodland that sat behind the estate.

"So, I have come to realise that, throughout these past few years – I have never asked you about your mother. I am so sorry that I never met her. What was her name?"

"Carolina", Rosa muttered. "I miss her very much. She died when I was ten years of age, it will be eighteen years this winter. She died giving birth to, what I was told, would have been my younger brother. I have resented that baby ever since. Even though its soul was taken just like my mother's was, I still hate it. At a time like this, I wish I had my mother's guidance. Not to say that I am not happy – I am. I truly am. I just wish I had her here to keep me strong."

Vicente was flummoxed. This had been the start of a conversation he hadn't quite prepared for. He knew that her mother had died, but had never quite practised in his head how to respond. "But you are strong, stronger and more beautiful than any woman I have ever come across. And my mother adores you. You have made her happy, which has been a rarity for many years now. I have never been so sure in my life that I want, no, need you to be my wife. You are the one thing that makes me whole." All of this, of course, was not entirely true. Vicente's adoration of his woman had blinded him to his mother's reaction every time he spoke of Rosa and how Lucia questioned, meticulously, every detail of her, through mistrust and suspicion.

Vicente strolled through the dry woodland, with Rosa's hand clutched firmly in his. Every step he made, with his long spindly legs, was a bounce of happiness. He couldn't quite describe his feelings for this woman, and if he could, would never utter them to his mother, who he was sure would think him a love sick fool. Which he was, he knew, but he couldn't help it. This woman had a hold on him and every sight of her filled Vicente with hope and joy.

"Oh Rosa! My beautiful woman! How I dream of our life after this wedding is over. How I waste days thinking of it while I should be slaving away in the field. What of our children? How many do you think we shall have? Three? Four? I hope most of them are boys. But of course we shall need one girl for you. No! Two! One will be called Lucia and the other Carolina. I hope that they are as beautiful as you are."

Rosa smiled in response and the fluffy conversation continued. Had he asked her the deepest secret that she possessed, would she have confessed? Probably not. A man, or rather child that she had loved from a younger age was still very deep in her heart. Though this man, who must have been at least thirty years of age by now, was a Felix. Leonardo Felix. A family name that was infamously known in the region. Known for killing Vicente's father and older brother. Although all three of them were extremely young when the murder occurred, mentioning this truth would have ruined everything, so she was relieved when, after the short walk, Vicente mounted his horse and rode off back to his mother, without any idea of Leonardo.

***

Later on that evening, one of the town's seamstresses came to the house, bearing a beautiful white dress, accompanied with a delicately embroided Mantilla head dress and comb. This woman, along with several maids of the house, danced around Rosa with joy, who sat in her bedroom as they fussed around her, hands clapped together in joy that their little Rosa was to be married and taken care of and two great houses of Andalucia would be united by this wedding, this anticipated occasion. All the excitement and flustering from the servants seemed a distant haze to Rosa, who showed little excitement, nor appreciation for the beautiful dress and adornments. In her mind raged a host of confused emotions and thoughts. She dared, for an instant, to think that maybe she didn't want any of this, maybe she didn't want marriage or betrothal. She tried to snap out of these thoughts. After all, the marriage would make her father extremely proud as it would have done with her mother too.

Seis.

Sure enough, the day of the wedding came. A hot day, like any other. The occasion took place in the town's Plaza Major, where the main church proudly produced the married couple with its bells ringing jubilantly and half the town seemed to come and celebrate the occasion. A mere street away was where the fiesta continued throughout the evening and into the night. The best taverna in town hosted the couple and their party. Vicente took his beautiful wife eagerly by the hand and led her through a rain of rice.

"I love you" was a phrase that was consistently on Vicente's lips. Initially, Rosa returned the gesture with a "I love you too" but this soon turned to a "I know" and a forced smile. He flaunted his wife like a prize, kissing her, dancing with her, offering her wine and food with his own hand, as if she was a naïve child.

The party progressed, both in the taverna and out in the street. A guitarist struck his instrument seductively with an accompanying female singer who wailed a deep, passionate melody while the audience clapped to the rhythm. Wine flowed like water and the town's people danced and drank themselves into a dizzy whirl. All the while, a mysterious figure peered into the party, focusing on one particular person, who seemed happy and content with her evening. His dark, beautiful eyes stared longingly at her, envious of her husband who bragged with her by his side. For years, this silhouette in the darkness had never been able to get this woman out of his mind. A woman who, unknowingly, held him back from truly embracing parenthood and his own marriage. A woman who he feared had forgotten all about him.

While the fiesta marched through the night, the parents, señor Machado and Lucia, sat at a table in mature calmness, saying little, but smiling happily at their children's good fortune.

"This is all I have ever wanted for my son", confessed Lucia, eyeing the couple as they danced. "He has guided me through hell and back and has never once shown himself as anything other than a loyal son to his mother. He is a saint in my eyes and the one thing that I hold dear in my life."

"I know, I know exactly how you must feel! My daughter has been such a great comfort to me since my wife passed away during child birth. In a way, she reminds me of all the good things of her. All the things that I loved about my wife."

"Your wife – dead. My husband – dead", Lucia replied. "We seem to have more in common that merely our children. Albeit in unfortunate circumstances. And we have used our children as crutches ever since. This is the night where we must find our own independence."

Señor Machado took a large swig of wine and dared to ask, "May I be blunt and pose the question as to how your husband died?"

"The house of Felix", she replied, speaking with raw hatred. "Behind bars and never to be released is not punishment enough for what they did to devastate my family. My husband and my eldest son were ripped away from me and if the Felix family was released it would give me pleasure to rip out their black hearts with my hands and watch their pain!"

Señor Machado was left feeling uneasy after listening to this woman's pure hate in her voice. Of course, she had every right to be hateful of the family name. He, however, fondly recalled a friendship which once his daughter had as a child with the youngest of the Felix family, Leonardo. This childhood friend now only had a wife and child, as his brothers and father were left in prison and his mother had also long since died. He remained silent.

***

It was late. Definitely after midnight, possibly an hour or two after. The night seemed to drag on so slowly for the new wife. Despite her confusion and the thousand different thoughts troubling her mind, Rosa tried not to show it.

"I need air", she confessed to Vicente. "Will you wait for me, I will only be gone a moment."

Vicente grinned innocently. "Of course, shall I come with you?"

"No, it's okay. I will not be gone long", she said. "I love you."

The temperature was no cooler outside than it was inside, but the deafening noise and excitement was becoming unbearable. She walked aimlessly along the street and into a neighbouring Plaza and rested on a bench that stood beside a lamp post. This Plaza wasn't as elegant as the town's main plaza, it didn't have an array of tavernas and restaurants, nor a magnificent fountain. Several young men stood underneath an archway that led into the plaza, smoke billowing from their cigarettes as they laughed and joked. She rested on the bench for some time, her eyes staring blankly at the floor. After a while, she became aware of someone else who came and sat beside her. Her heart pounded in her chest, with nerves and excitement, echoing that of the man who decided to take a seat next to her. Then a firm hand took hers and said, "Rosa. I love you. I always have."

"Leonardo, stop! I beg you, please. This is too late. Far too late. I have seen you outside my bedroom window most nights. You confuse me so much. My head has been toiling with the thoughts of you. I cannot believe I am even confessing this – and that you're telling me that you love me today – today of all days. Why now?"

Leonardo looked passionately into her eyes and then down to her lips.

"If I never told you I couldn't forgive myself. My feelings have always remained the same."

As the couple dared to confess their love for one another, a silhouette watched from the darkness of her bedroom, which overlooked the plaza, now empty except for her husband and this woman that the whole town was celebrating. As Leonardo leaned in to kiss this bride, his wife clasped her hand to her mouth to stifle her cry. At this point the couple ran from the Plaza, hands gripped together in an embrace of passion.

One of the young men that had been smoking in the archway had remained to incidentally witness the kiss. As soon as they had fled he raced back through the paved streets and into the party and exclaimed to everyone there: "Vicente I have seen your wife kissing Leonardo, Leonardo Felix, and they have just ran from the town."

The entire room fell completely silent. Señor Machado shook his head with disbelief and shame.

"What?! No! Not my daughter. This isn't true, my daughter is a good girl. This fool must be mistaken!"

"This fool is not mistaken, señor", Lucia snapped back. "A Felix? A Felix? What kind of insult is this? I should have known. I should have known – I feel so foolish. Vicente, listen to me", she turned to her son, who was stunned and shocked, and fiercely kissed his forehead, then said, "You ignorant boy! You should have known better. But we were both blinded by her beauty and her father's promises. Avenge me – and avenge yourself. A horse! Quick! Someone give my son a horse!"

Several men came forward from the party's crowd and offered both horses and their help.

"All of you hunt them both down. Shake the dust from your shoes. Go help my son. Take every road. Search the forest. The hour of blood is here once more!"

The whole taverna emptied in a drunken, heated rage – leaving señor Machado slumped in his chair – speechless. Before leaving as the last person from the taverna, Lucia turned and, with disgust, glared at the helpless, old father.

"I have been through so much with my son, and this shameless daughter of yours has done her best to destroy any pride that we both have. I do not pity the shame you must be feeling right now. You bore a heartless child who tricked me into believing she was good enough for my Vicente."

Siete.

Other than the loud screech of the cicadas and the long grass rustling under foot, the lover's flustered and quickened breath echoed through the forest that lay in the valley between the town and the mountains, heading north. They envisioned a stampede of townsfolk following their footsteps with knives and pistols and ravenous dogs that tugged at their leads. The sun had not yet reached the horizon, yet the woodland was becoming more and more visible. The moon, like an onlooker, still hung in the sky watching the lovers as they ran in fear of their lives.

All of a sudden, Rosa let go of Leonardo's hand and gasped for air, as each side of her torso throbbed with pain. She slumped to the ground and wept.

"What have I done?", She asked rhetorically. "I have turned my husband's love into pure hate! For what? For my longing and yearning for you! I feel so ashamed."

She clapped her hands to her face and sobbed. Leonardo, however, stood above her for a short while and then slowly lowered himself to her level and took both her hands in his.

"I don't feel ashamed. I don't feel at all ashamed. My love for you is stronger than any shame and I know that you feel the same too. You had a choice, and you chose me. This makes me feel the most loved man in all of Spain. I don't care about our life before. I don't care about any of it. I am so sorry that I left you all those years when I should have spoken the truth with my feelings when things would have been easier. I love you. I love you with every fibre of my body. I always have. And I feel no shame. We can start a new. In Sevilla, in Madrid, in America – anywhere. Our life can start a new. No one need know of our past. You will make me the happiest man and I assure you I'd make you the happiest wife. Kiss me, please. Kiss me to show me that you understand and feel the same."

With that, Rosa threw herself into Leonardo's arms and they kissed passionately. In the depth of the forest that sprawled across the valley they had happened across a clearing, with mere shrubbery and low lying foliage to keep them cover. Rosa lay down, staring up at Leonardo whose sturdy, sun bleached arms held him up above her whilst the moon's light caressed his back as they held one another, completely exposed and in sight of Vicente's devastated eyes.

Rosa buried her face into Leonardo's muscular chest, filled with the passion of the night, along with the fear and shame of what had happened, but felt safe in his arms – believing that nothing could harm them.

Vicente did nothing for quite a while. Stunned and enraged by what he saw, he couldn't quite believe how easily he had been tricked by the love of his life. Rage flowed through his body until he couldn't take any more. He ran towards the embraced couple and ripped Leonardo off his bride. No words were exchanged. Everything seemed to happen so fast for Rosa who lay terrified on the floor. Both men took out small daggers from their pockets and threw themselves at each other, the sharp blades piercing the skin of both men simultaneously. Both Vicente and Leonardo let out a cry of intense pain and blood gushed out of each one's wounds, Leonardo's placed in his gut and Vicente's straight into his heart. Vicente collapsed almost instantly while Leonardo held his balance and, turning to Rosa, tried to stagger towards her. She raced to him and caught him as he fell into her and shivered with the pain that he felt. Vicente was already dead, with blood soaking the forest floor.

Rosa kissed Leonardo painfully on the lips but received no response, she opened her eyes to see him staring blindly past her, up at the moon that still hung in the air, a witness to the slaughter. Rosa wailed as she rocked Leonardo gently in her arms. She heard voices approaching in reaction to her cry. She slowly lay Leonardo down on the floor, took one look at her husband and burst into an uncontrollable scream which brought about more murmurs that came ever closer to the scene. She had no choice – she doubled back and threw herself into the thicket of pine trees and up into the mountain.

El Fin.

Several days passed. Many tears drowned the eyes of those affected as wine had poured in jubilation not even a week ago, both for the same man - Vicente. Only his wife, a recluse in her shabby house, wept for Leonardo.

The following Thursday afternoon Lucia could be found in a small chapel in between her house and the town which stood on a mound accompanied by several pine trees and a cemetery that lay behind it. In this cemetery a new grave had been freshly dug, next to her eldest son and husband.

Pride kept Lucia from weeping, at least not in the eyes of others – she had already been proven weak enough by believing that the whore could be good enough for Vicente.

She knelt in the chapel, with its simple white washed interior and a giant crucifix with Jesus agonised with pain mounted in the centre by the altar, his eyes showing his suffering while blood trickled down from his scalp.

She did little more than blink and stare at the tiled floor, her head racked with hatred, grief and fury.

On this Thursday afternoon, the rains finally came to Andalucia to bring relief back to the people of the town and the surrounding parched land. The raindrops clattered on the roof of the chapel as intuition brought a particular woman into the sacred place, soaking wet and dressed in a dirty, dry-blooded, drenched, white dress. She had been hesitant to confront Lucia for several days – aware that she was the reason for these two deaths. Above the land the skies were ripped apart by a storm and lightening dashed through the clouds.

Rosa's presence at the altar, crossing herself and kneeling in front of the crucifix, brought all the rage and anger that Lucia had within her up into her mouth.

"How dare you show your face here, or anywhere near this town?", Lucia said behind clenched teeth. "How do you find the nerve to do so?"

In the grieving mother's mind, Rosa should have been found and left for dead on the dusty plains. Yet again, no – a life of self loathing and guilt would surely be a better price to pay.

"Señora – there are no words that I can start to say to explain my feelings and my sorrow."

"Sorrow?", Lucia cracked. "Pha! A whore feels no sorrow, a whore feels nothing. Why do you continue to lie to me like this. There is no need. Your deeds are done here. You have taken from an old woman everything that she had left and the decent thing you could possibly do now is run, as fast as you can, before I tell all the townspeople to hunt you down."

All this was spoken while Lucia continued to look down at the floor. The sight of this woman would anger her so much that she couldn't have possibly contained herself from striking Rosa, as she felt she deserved – and possibly wouldn't stop until she was a bloodied mess on the chapel floor.

"Indeed you must know, I am pure. I know it does little for your grief, but Leonardo had done nothing with me that night and for that I remain your son's wife."

Lucia, raised her eyes from the floor and glared at the woman. "What does that matter to me? Intentions are intentions. If you hadn't have loved that Felix boy you would be in a bed somewhere, miles from here – reproducing unfortunate mistakes and acts you'd call 'love'. You deserve everything that is coming to you!"

"No more. No more! Take your revenge; here I am", Rosa said bravely. "Look how tender my throat is; it would cost you less effort to cut it than to cut a flower in a garden. If you were to light a fire, right this instant we'd put our hands into its flames; you for your son, I, for my body. You'll be the first to withdraw, for I promise you I am pure."

"What does your purity matter to me? What does your death matter?", Lucia questioned. "Just get out!".

Rosa stood strong in her belief in her purity and her right to grieve.

"No, señora, I shall stay, I have to say all I need to say."

"There is no more to say. GET OUT!"

Rosa didn't flinch, and with that the old woman, with the last ounce of force she had left in her body, lunged at the young girl and dragged her out of the chapel, throwing her out of the doors violently. Rosa tumbled down the flight of steps that led up to the doorway. Lucia spat after her, "If I ever see you in this town again, I promise you I shall rip out your eyes and burrow my teeth into your neck. As will anyone within a one hundred mile radius from here. You are not welcome. I'm sure even your father would spit at the sight of you", and with that she slammed the door behind her.

Rosa was shaken from what had just occurred and winded by the fall from the chapel. She looked around, yet no one had witnessed what had happened – fortunately, as she felt ashamed and had done all she could to apologise for any sin that she had committed. But Rosa knew that was the last possible opportunity she had and, with that, picked herself up and clumsily ran, in no specific direction, away from the town, her father, Lucia, everyone – over the plains and out of sight.

Printed in Great Britain
by Amazon